THE AMAZING SPIDER-MAN™

BEWARE the LIZARD!

ADAPTED BY
NACHIE CASTRO

BASED ON THE MOTION PICTURE SCREENPLAY WRITTEN BY
JAMES VANDERBILT

MARVEL
NEW YORK

MARVEL SPIDER-MAN MERCHANDISING COLUMBIA PICTURES

Published by Marvel Press, an imprint of Disney Book Group. No part of this book may
be reproduced or transmitted in any form or by any means, electronic or mechanical,
including photocopying, recording, or by any information storage and retrieval system,
without written permission from the publisher. For information address Marvel Press,
114 Fifth Avenue, New York, New York 10011-5690.

Printed in the United States of America

First Edition

1 3 5 7 9 10 8 6 4 2

G658-7729-4-12106

ISBN 978-1-4231-5479-2

PETER PARKER HAD ONLY BEEN SPIDER-MAN
for a short time. Yet he had already met the fiercest
villain the world had ever seen—the monster known
as the Lizard! But Spider-Man knew there was more
to the Lizard than just a rampaging beast.

THE LIZARD had once been the brilliant scientist Dr. Curtis Connors. Dr. Connors worked at the scientific-research company Oscorp. He knew Peter Parker and had even worked with Peter's father! Many years ago, Dr. Connors lost his right arm in an accident.

DR. CONNORS HAD ALWAYS DREAMED of finding a way to get his arm back. He had been working on an experimental formula, based on the regenerative abilities of some reptiles. But he couldn't get it to work. One day, while talking to Peter Parker, Dr. Connors had a new idea!

ONCE DR. CONNORS had figured out the missing piece of the puzzle, he quickly got to work on his formula. He was very close to finally being able to grow his arm back, and he wasn't going to let anything get in his way!

ONCE THE FORMULA WAS READY, Dr. Connors hid in his lab. He knew that he would get in trouble if anyone found him, but he also knew that sometimes scientists had to take risks.

DR. CONNORS WATCHED IN AWE as his right arm grew back! His attempt to introduce the reptile's ability for regeneration to human DNA had worked!

AT FIRST, DR. CONNORS WAS THRILLED!

Not only had he been able to help himself, but he knew this formula could help other people all across the world. He started preparing his notes. But all of a sudden, he started to feel strange. . . .

THE FORMULA HAD SUCCEEDED in combining the reptile DNA with Dr. Connors's DNA, but it did more than just heal his arm. It changed him into a half-man, half-reptile. And where Dr. Connors wanted to help people, this new creature only wanted to destroy! He was no longer human, he was only **THE LIZARD!**

CAPTAIN STACY, head of a special police unit, was called to stop the Lizard's rampage through New York! The police did everything they could, but the Lizard was too powerful.

SPIDER-MAN KNEW he had to stop the Lizard, but he also knew that he didn't want to hurt Dr. Connors! He swung into action, but he was worried that he wouldn't be able to win the day.

PETER WAS ABLE TO HOLD THE LIZARD at bay long enough for the Lizard to change back into Dr. Connors, but the fight was tough! Dr. Connors hadn't been completely lost within the Lizard, but he could tell that the monster could take control again at any moment. He needed Spider-Man's help!

WOULD PETER PARKER AND DR. CONNORS

be able to come up with a cure before Dr. Connors turned into the Lizard once more? No matter what happened, one thing was certain—Spider-Man wouldn't give up on Dr. Connors, no matter the odds!